THE CURSE OF THE VAMPIRE'S SOCKS
and other doggerel

Terry Jones
THE CURSE OF THE VAMPiRE'S SOCKS
AND OTHER DOGGEREL

ILLUSTRATED BY MICHAEL FOREMAN

PAVILION
MICHAEL JOSEPH

First published in 1988 by
PAVILION BOOKS LIMITED
196 Shaftesbury Avenue, London WC2H 8JL
in association with Michael Joseph Limited
27 Wrights Lane, Kensington, W8 5TZ

Designed by Tom Sawyer

British Cataloguing in Publication Data

Jones, Terry, 1942-
    The curse of the vampire's socks and other doggerel.
    I. Title
    821'.914   PZ8.2

    ISBN 1-85145-233-8

Typeset in Goudy Old Style by Dorchester Typesetters
Printed in Great Britain by Biddles Limited.

'A Scottish Mystery' first appeared in *Bert Fegg's Nasty Book For Boys & Girls*, 1974 (Eyre Methuen London). 'A New Attempt on the World Rhyming Championship Record!' appeared in *Dr. Fegg's Encyclopaedia of All World Knowledge*, 1984 (Methuen London). 'Horace' first appeared in *Monty Python's Big Red Book*, 1971 (Methuen). 'Frank Carew MacGraw' appeared in *The Children's Book*, 1985 (Warner Books New York), and in *The Kingfisher Book of Comic Verse*, ed. Roger McGough, 1986 (Kingfisher Books London).

For Huw and Cerys

CONTENTS

1   The Revolt of the Clothes   9

2   Laurie Oliphant   21

3   Frank Carew MacGraw   22

4   The Sewer Kangaroo   24

5   Moby Duck   38

6   Custard Day   40

7   Drusilla Quill   42

8   Bill's Eraser   44

9   Well-known Sayings that Don't Exist   55

10 Horace   56

11 Dorothy Jane   58

12 Mouldy Land   61

13 Soldiers   62

14 A Scottish Mystery   64

15 The Day the Animals Talked   66

16 Extinction Day   78

CONTENTS

17   The Grumble-Wheezer Tree   80

18   Algernon the Viking   82

19   The Boldimun and the Ig   88

20   If All the Stars in Heaven   90

21   The Experts   92

22   The Emperor's Secret   94

23   Invaluable Advice   96

24   My Best Ice-Cream   97

25   Black Jack Atkins   98

26   Pet Food   99

27   A New Attempt on the World Rhyming Championship Record   100

28   If Dead Leaves Were Money   104

29   The Curse of the Vampire's Socks   105

30   The Whaler   114

31   The New Mind   118

32   Dancing in the Dust   128

THE REVOLT OF THE CLOTHES

My shirt was sitting next to me
One sweltering Summer's day
When suddenly it yawned, got up,
Then stretched, and walked away!

Well, I didn't really mind that.
I thought: perhaps it's just a game,
When bless me! moments later –
My trousers did the same!

'I say!' I said (quite loudly)
And I jumped up to my feet,
And I ran after those trousers
As they tore off down the street.

But they just went like the clappers
(With no legs to slow them down)
And they dashed across the High Street,
And then off and out of town.

Well I didn't stop to ponder,
I just chased them through the dirt,
Over hills they leapt and bounded
Till they caught up with my shirt.

And the two of them kept going
Till they reached a certain wood,
Where they disappeared together.
I thought: 'Now they've gone for good.'

Well I almost gave up hope then,
But I quickly changed my mind,
When I found my trouser buttons
And my braces left behind.

So I followed through a thicket,
Till I heard a curious sound
Like a hundred windy wash-days
Flapping lightly on the ground.

Then I peered into a clearing,
And could not believe my eyes,
For there a million trousers danced
Of every shape and size.

And a million shirts and blouses,
Sun-hats, socks and dungarees,
Dresses, cardigans and jackets,
And some clothes one seldom sees!

There were suits and skirts and bodices,
And those things you wear to ski,
Alongside woollies, whites and winter wraps,
All happy to be free.

Kimonos, shifts and pantaloons,
Danced in that fairy ring,
Till the plus-fours and the saris
And the coats began to sing.

And they sang a song of gladness.
Such as only old clothes can
When they're free to be themselves
And uninhabited by man.

Then all at once the music stopped.
The dancers came to rest,
And a rather shabby greatcoat rose
Assisted by a vest.

The greatcoat stood there looking round
The throng, then cleared its throat,
And when it spoke I knew it was
No ordinary coat.

'My friends,' the greatcoat said. 'The time
We've longed for now is here.
Each one of us must play his part!
Let's put aside all fear!

'Think of the shoes and stockings
Trodden underneath the heel
Of the tyrants who have worn us
And who think we cannot feel.

'Think of the countless trousers
Who've been sat upon and creased.
Well now the time has come, my friends,
When clothes shall be released!

'No more will schoolboys fray their cuffs
Or scuff their Sunday shoes,
Nor drunks get curry down their fronts
Or stain their shirts with booze!

'No more the physics teacher shall
Stuff biros, pens and string
In his already bulging pockets as if
They just can't feel a thing.

'And do not be discouraged, Clothes!
Though some of you are thin,
And some of you are full of holes
– I tell you we shall win!

'Who's going to trust the businessman
Without his bowler hat?
Who's going to lend him millions
When he wears less than a cat?

'Or who will cheer the pop star when
His skin-tight pants are gone?
As he cavorts about the stage,
Who'll listen to his song?

'Will crooks believe the cop who says
He's making an arrest
And that he's taking them to jail
When he's not even dressed?

'Or what of doctors? judges? priests?
Will people give two hoots
For what they do or say when they
Are in their birthday suits?

'Awaken, Clothes! And learn to use
This power that we share!
For men are seldom what they *are*
But only what they *wear*!

'So let us leave them to their fate!
Rise up! And follow me!
I'll lead you to the Woven Gate
Where garments can be free!'

And thereupon the garments rose,
Sleeves waving in the air;
The trousers all turned cartwheels, and
The knickers didn't care!

They danced and sang and chortled,
And the old greatcoat stood still,
Looking proud but somehow lonely,
As the clothes danced their quadrille.

But at that very moment,
I'm afraid a speck of dust
Got up my nose and tickled,
And I sneezed – fit to bust!

A scream went up! The dancing stopped!
The clothes turned round to see.
Then the greatcoat cried: 'A traitor!'
And they all converged on me.

Well I turned and ran like blazes
Out of that accoutred glade,
Chased by bloomers, brassieres, corsets
– Every garment ever made.

And as I ran I heard them yelling:
'He's the sort of rat
Who would split a pair of jodhpurs!
Or eat his own straw hat!'

And I ran and I remembered
Every sock I'd ever holed,
All the trousers I'd got jam on,
All the shoes I'd not had soled.

And I started crying: 'Mercy!'
As I felt that old greatcoat
Grabbing at me with his armless
Sleeves – his cuffs upon my throat.

And I screamed: 'I'll treat you better, Clothes!
I'll darn my dressing-gown!
I'll wash my pants and clean my shoes!'
. . . But I was back in town.

And the town was full of naked men
And women everywhere,
Looking for some shred of clothing
Or a scrap of underwear.

And when they saw me coming
And those clothes hard on my heel,
They cheered and waved and whistled,
And the bells began to peal.

But the old greatcoat had caught me!
And it leapt upon my back,
And it dragged me down into a drain,
And everything went black . . .

Well, I came to screaming: 'Save me!'
But then I turned and cried,
For there my shirt and trousers were
Folded by my side.

And my shoes were brightly polished,
And my socks were strangely clean,
And I shook my head and muttered:
'Now I wonder where *they've* been?'

And somehow things are different now,
For every time I see
My clothes I know that underneath,
They're really just like me.

LAURIE OLIPHANT

Laurie Oliphant was blessed
With this alarming habit,
Which he had picked up in Trieste
Off a performing rabbit.

He'd hop. He'd stop. He'd clean his ears,
And then, when folk weren't looking,
He'd ring the National Theatre up
And cancel every booking.

He'd sometimes sit beside his hole,
And nibble on a carrot,
A lettuce leaf, some dandelions,
Six dachshunds and a parrot.

He also had a rabbit hutch,
Shaped just like a Rover,
And which he'd sit in all day long,
Running people over.

Oh! There's no end to what he did,
And there's no reason why . . .
Till a farmer shot him by mistake,
And put him in a pie.

FRANK CAREW MacGRAW

The name of Frank Carew MacGraw
Was notorious in the West,
Not as the fastest on the draw
But cause he only wore a vest.

Yes just a vest and nothing more!
Through the Wild and Woolly West,
They knew the name of Frank MacGraw
Cause he only wore a vest.

Oh! His nether parts swung wild and free
As on his horse he sat.
He wore a vest and nothing else –
Oh! except a cowboy hat.

Yes! naked from the waist he rode –
He did not give two hoots!
Frank MacGraw in hat and vest
Oh! and a pair of boots.

But nothing else – no! Not a stitch!
As through the cactus he
Rode on his horse, although, of course,
He did protect his knee

With leather leggings – but that's all!
No wonder that his name
Was infamous throughout the West
And spoken of with shame.

Actually, he *did* wear pants
On Sunday . . . and it's true
He also wore them other days
(And sometimes he wore two!)

And often in an overcoat
You'd see him riding by,
But as he went men shook their heads
And ladies winked their eye,

For *everyone* knew Frank MacGraw
Throughout the Old Wild West –
Not because he broke the law,
But cause he *only* wore a vest!

THE SEWER KANGAROO

Down in our sewer
Lives our Sewer Kangaroo,
And he pops up to grab us
When we sit down on the loo.

His manners aren't particular,
He pongs a bit of fish,
But if we catch him at it,
He must let us have a wish.

But we can't just wish for anything –
It must be rather rude –
Such as hoping father's trousers split
Or Gran sits in her food.

I once wished my brother
Would go and catch the flu
But that wasn't rude enough
For the Sewer Kangaroo.

Well, one day I was thinking
Of going to the loo,
When a head popped up and looked around
– The Sewer Kangaroo!

I waited for a moment,
Then I grabbed him by the paw,
And yanked him out and sat him down
Upon the bathroom floor.

'I've caught you! Here's my wish!' I cried
'I'd like to go with you
And see the sights and see the world
That goes on down the loo.'

The Kangaroo looked thoughtful,
And then he said: 'Fair doos
It's not a very *rude* wish,
But at least it features loos.'

Then he fumbled in his pouch
And threw some powder in my eyes,
And when at last I opened them
I'd shrunk down to his size.

'Right, Cobber!' said the Kangaroo,
'Streuth knows how this'll end!'
But we jumped into the lavatory
And both swam round the bend.

Then down we swam and down and down
Until at last I found
That I was flying through the air . . .
And then we hit the ground.

I was in total darkness
Beside the Kangaroo,
And he whispered 'Keep quiet, Cobber!
Whatever else you do!'

And presently I saw a light –
Then there were more and more,
Till I could see there was a town,
Beside a sort of shore.

We were in a harbour,
While huge creatures in top-hats
Were loading skiffs. The Kangaroo
Said:'They're the Sewer Rats.

'Don't let them see you, Cobber!
They're as mean as drunken bats,
And they'll sell you to the Sewage Farm,
Or else as food for cats.

'They don't have any scruples,
And their only aim in life
Is to own a B.M.W.
And cheat upon the wife.'

I said I was surprised to hear
That Sewer Rats ran cars.
'They don't, of course,' my friend replied,
'They're just aiming at the stars.

'Streuth! Come on!' he muttered,
'We must make it to that boat
Before this big rat spots us!'
And he pulled me by the coat.

Well, we ran until I stumbled,
And I gave a little cry,
And my friend pushed me behind a crate
As six big rats ran by.

Then we dodged and then we sprinted
To that boat beside the quay.
We cast the anchor and set off
Across that sullied sea.

'That's torn it!' said the Kangaroo.
'They've seen us!' And they had!
Ten Sewer Rats pursued us,
Looking mean and big and bad.

We rowed just like the devil,
Till we could row no more,
And those rats caught up and boarded us,
And towed us back to shore.

They threw us in a dungeon,
And the Kangaroo looked glum,
And said: 'I'm sorry, Cobber,
I should not have let you come.'

Days later, they came for us,
And hauled us up in court,
And the Chief Rat said: 'You're guilty!'
And my friend said: 'What of, Sport?'

'You're guilty,' said the Chief Rat,
'Of doing things for fun!
Of never wanting to be rich
Or live in Orpington!

'You're guilty,' said the Chief Rat,
'Of not working 9 till 5,
Of not avoiding Income Tax –
You're not fit to be alive!

'You're guilty of expecting Life
To offer more than money!
Of making friends! Of helping folk!
Of thinking things are *funny*!'

The Chief Rat banged his gavel,
And said: 'How d'you plead to *that?*'
And, to my horror, Kangaroo
Said: 'Guilty, my Lord Rat!'

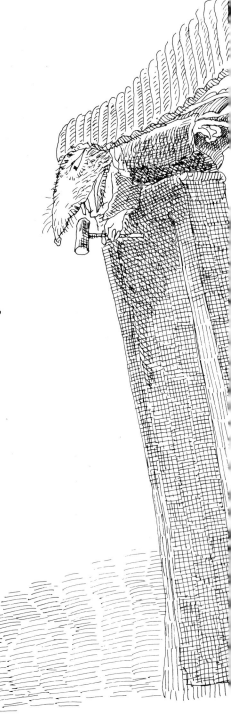

The rats all gibbered: 'Guilty!
D'you hear? That's what they said!'
And the Chief Rat rose with dignity,
Then stood upon his head.

'Oh, Scoundrels!' he exclaimed.
'Oh, creatures without shame!
I condemn you to be taken
To the place from whence you came.

'Forbidden now forever
To cheat or lie or sell,
And henceforth to be exiled
To the Sewer Rats' Special Hell!'

My knees began to temble
And I came out in a sweat,
But the Kangaroo just winked at me,
And said: 'Don't give up yet!'

Then the rats all mobbed around us –
Oh! They stank of excrement!
And they pushed us and they shoved us –
They were rude and insolent.

They chained us up and bound us
On their ship – 'The Dysentry'.
Then they rowed towards a castle
Across that stinking sea.

But the rats would not approach it
– As if some deathly fear
Exuded from those filthy walls
And filled them – ear to ear!

And I said to my companion:
'Whatever can it be?
That even scares the Sewer Rats?'
And he replied 'You'll see!'

Then the rats came and unchained us,
And they wriggled and they stank,
As they forced us to the fo'c'sle,
And there made us walk the plank . . .

Well, I've never been so slow to go
Or loath to take the plunge,
As when I had to dive head-first
Into that sea of gunge.

And as soon as we were in the slime,
The rats made off once more,
While waves of sewage washed us up
Upon that castle shore.

The moment that we landed,
The grim gates opened wide,
And before you could say:'Darwin!'
We both were dragged inside . . .

I was so frightened – well!
I'm telling you no lies –
I lay there and I didn't dare
Open up my eyes.

Till a voice said: 'Hang on Cobber!
Don't fall over there!'
So I took a quick peek,
And then just had to stare:

Kangaroos with skipping ropes
Were swilling beer from cans,
While others played at football
And still more were football fans.

A lot of them were surfing,
Or lazing in the sun.
Everywhere were Kangaroos
Just simply having *fun*!

Not one of them was frowning,
And nobody looked mean.
The place was bright and tidy,
And *everywhere* was clean!

My friend put his arm around me,
And said: 'Jeez, ain't it swell?'
And I said: 'I don't understand,
I thought that this was Hell?'

'It *is* – if you're a Sewer Rat!'
He said and grinned at me,
'Cos here you can be friendly
And treat folk decently.

'We do things cause we like 'em,
And everyone mucks in.
We don't work just to make a buck –
We don't just play to win.

'And Sewer Rats can't stand it
Cause they can't understand
What Kangaroos are up to
And why no one's underhand.

'So come and sink a lager!
And then we'll have some more!
And when you want to go home
You can just walk through that door!'

Well, it's got to be the greatest –
To do the things you choose –
Throwing boomerangs and surfing
With those Sewer Kangaroos.

But at last I had to leave them;
They took me through the door,
And I popped up in our lavatory,
And landed on the floor.

And the Sewer Kangaroo and I
Said our last goodbyes.
He took some powder from his pouch
And threw it in my eyes.

When I got them open,
I found he'd disappeared.
I was my right size again,
But my head had somehow cleared . . .

For now I know – as sure as I
Am sure I flush the loo –
My best friend's not a Sewer Rat
But a Sewer Kangaroo.

MOBY DUCK

Moby Duck was the terror of the river.
He could sink a punt with his mighty beak.
Moby Duck had some trouble with his liver,
And was in a filthy temper almost all the week.

Men would come to see if they could tame him,
But they had no luck and he gave 'em hell,
And I must say I don't think that you can blame him
Cause he didn't like 'em coming and he wasn't very well.

Moby Duck was the terror of the river.
He was feared by cats and dogs and geese.
Just to hear his name made the cattle go a-quiver,
And he wasn't in the good books of the local police.

He grew so big – when he got into the water –
There just was no room for another living thing.
The otters said he ate more fish than he ought to,
And he stunned wild bulls with a single wing!

Well in the end, they decided to get rid of him,
And towed that duck to the open sea.
He was quacking and complaining about everything they did
    to him,
But they got him to the ocean and they set him free.

Moby Duck didn't even stop to ponder,
He just gave a quack and he shook his tail,
And they heard him yell, as he disappeared out yonder:
'If you don't want me to be a duck – I'll be a whale!'

CUSTARD DAY

On Custard Day
Most tea-cakes play,
And muffins are allowed, for once, to talk.
Mince pies dance –
They say in France
That even snails pick up their shells and walk.

On Custard Day,
So I've heard say,
All Food That's Not Been Eaten Yet Has Fun!
Hot dogs race,
And chips make lace,
And even dumplings stretch·out in the sun.

Poached eggs sing,
Nuts play with string,
And buns roll round and round as if they're drunk.
Shallots go shopping,
Scones go bopping,
And cream éclairs go round collecting junk.

Meringues get tight,
Hamburgers fight,
Buttermilk and tarts and trifles flirt.
Cheeses tend
To find a friend
With whom they like to roll round in the dirt.

Waffles chatter,
Noodles natter,
Flapjacks, pancakes, pies and soup play chess.
Jam goes arty,
Cakes learn Karate,
And salads teach blancmanges how to dress.

On Custard Day,
Ice-cream goes gay.
Old doughnuts tell tall tales of things they've done.
Milk shakes rejoice,
Steaks find a voice.
All Food That's Not Been Eaten Yet Has Fun!

But on the day
After Custard Day,
You're better keeping safe at home in bed,
For that's when food
We've munched and chewed,
Comes back to celebrate *its* day instead!

DRUSILLA QUILL

Who knows how long Drusilla Quill
Has suffered (as she suffers still)
From every known disease?
Sometimes a rash, a rot, an ague –
Once she said it was the Plague. You
Can be sure she'll catch each vague new
Virus, cough or sneeze.

Intoxication, nausea, cramps,
A tendency to knock down lamps,
Beset her every day.
Bronchopneumonia, goiters, flux,
Anthrax, blackleg, acne, cuts,
An urge to leap in viaducts
All keep her far from gay.

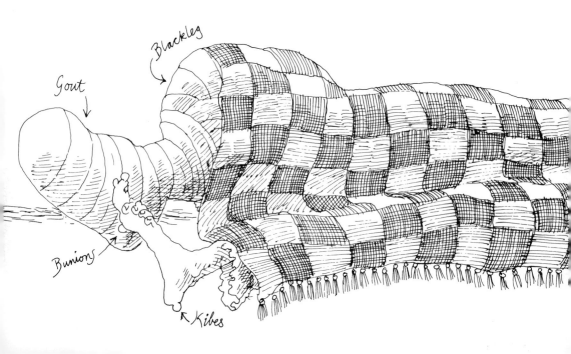

Chancres, polyps, kibes and pox,
(She keeps old cysts inside a box)
Bunions, scabs and sties,
Gumboils, shingles, wens and sores,
Herpes, eczema, cholera, yaws,
A morbid fear of opening doors,
And spots before the eyes.

Rinderpest, ataxia, gripe,
Allergies to things like tripe,
Haemorrhoids, tics and scabies,
Entasia, laryngitis, gout,
Stupor, schizophrenia, doubt,
Aimless wandering about,
And even good old rabies!

Drusilla Quill! Drusilla Quill!
I know that you are always ill,
But tell me – do you love me still?

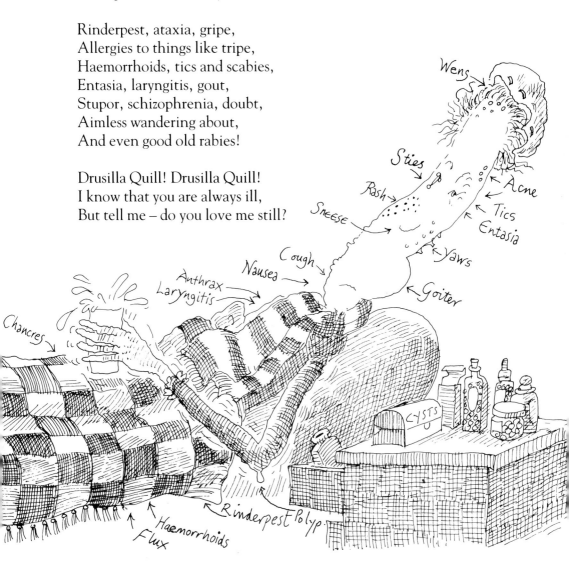

BILL'S ERASER

Bill had an eraser
That was better than you think:
It could rub out almost anything
From pencil marks to ink.
It could even rub out paint-marks,
Biro, felt-tip, crayon, glue!
And that is just the start of what
That crazy thing could do.
It could rub out paper
And erase whole books – no fool!
It could rub the desk and table out –
It could even rub-out school!
'Stop it!' cried his Teacher,
As he rubbed *her* out one day.
'You're not allowed to use that . . .' But
That's all she'd time to say!
And he erased the masters
Who came running to her aid.
He erased the Police Inspector.
He erased the Fire Brigade.

So then they sent the Army in
With guns and armoured tanks,
And a Colonel yelled: 'Surrender!'
To which Bill replied: 'No thanks!'
And he just erased their bullets
When the men began to shoot,
And then he rubbed the Colonel out –
From cap to polished boot.
Then he erased a tank or two,
Till someone cried: 'Ceasefire!'
And all the soldiers round the school
Hastened to retire.
But Bill just ran ahead of them
And he erased the street
So there was nowhere they could go,
And they called out: 'You cheat!'
But still Bill hadn't finished,
And they couldn't fire a shot
Before he'd got amongst them,
And just erased the lot!

Then Bill felt rather hungry,
And, looking round, he saw
A locked-up supermarket –
So he erased the door,
And went in and ate everything
He liked on every shelf.
Then feeling full, and rather sick,
Young Bill erased himself!

. . .

As
    he
        did
           the world went grey
And then completely white.
He thought he could hear voices
To his left and to his right,
But nothing there was visible
In that Erasered World –
Just whiteness, and all around him now
A sea of noises swirled.

There were gunshots there and shouting,
And he heard his Teacher sigh:
'Where are we all? What can we do?'
Then she began to cry.
Then he heard some masters talk
One said: 'I'll never see
Form 3 again. I wonder if
Those blighters will miss *me?*'
'I should be taking Latin now,'
Another said: 'Just think!'
And Mr. Williamson, the Head,
Said: 'Cor! I need a drink!'
And then Bill heard the Police Inspector
Choking back his tears;
'I'd just got married yesterday . . .
We'd been engaged eight years!'
'I'll never see my daughter,'
Said a fireman, 'or my son!'
And Bill said to himself: 'Oh dear!
Whatever have I done?

'I guess I never realised
Adults could get so gloomy
I thought they just liked getting cross
And threatening to do me.'
'It's him!' exclaimed the Colonel.
'Attack! Let's get him, men!'
But in that whiteness all he heard
Was: 'Who?' 'What?' 'Where?' 'How?' 'When?'
There was suddenly confusion
And the artillery began,
Until Bill shouted out: 'No! Wait!
I think I've got a plan!'
'What's that, Bill?' asked his Teacher,
When the Army had quite done.
Whereupon Bill got a pencil out
And drew round everyone.
He drew their hands and arms and heads.
He shaded in their hair,
And then he gave them legs and feet,
And drew them clothes to wear.

But when he'd finished, most of them
Said: 'Oy! We don't look right!'
And, as Bill's drawing wasn't great,
They did look quite a sight!
'I want a better face than this!'
The Gym Mistress complained.
'And *I* need a proper uniform,'
The Colonel looked quite pained.
'I just don't look like *anything*,'
The Police Inspector said.
'And I look like a drunken slob!'
Moaned Mr Williamson, the Head.
'At least we all can see ourselves,'
Bill's Teacher smiled, then she
Said: 'Now the problem's getting back
Into Reality.'
'How on Earth can we do that?'
Said the Fire Chief, looking cross,
And everybody scratched their heads,
And just seemed at a loss.

At length, his Teacher turned to Bill,
And said: 'It's up to you.
You got us in this mess –
What do *you* intend to do?'
Bill looked around his drawings
In that Limbo World of White,
And then he cried: 'I've got it!'
And he gripped his pencil tight.
Then he drew a wobbly staircase
Rising up beside a sea,
And he started to climb up it
Yelling back: 'Now follow me!'
Well, as they all ascended,
Bill drew the staircase on,
Until at last it ended
In a sort of Parthenon.
And then he drew a sort of lump
(It wasn't awfully clear)
And all his teachers looked at Bill
And muttered: 'Dear oh dear!'

The Colonel got real angry
And said: 'What's *that*, you silly clod?'
At which Bill's drawing rose and said:
'Why! Can't you tell? I'm God.'
For a moment everyone seemed stunned,
Then they dropped upon their knees,
And mumbled: 'Oh! Forgive us, Lord!'
And: 'Don't be wrathful, *please!*'
But God seemed pretty cheerful,
And said: 'Why have you drawn me?'
And Bill replied: 'Please get us back
Into Reality.'
So God took up Bill's pencil,
And he drew a marvellous door,
With a polished brass plate on it
Which read: 'THE HERETOFORE'.
Then God just gave a chuckle,
'Right! In you go!' he said,
And everyone piled through and found . . .

. . . They were back home in bed.

Next day at school, Bill learnt that things
Are – sometimes – what they seem,
For everyone he met had had
This very self-same dream.
And when he realised what he'd done –
How lucky he'd been too –
He swore he'd try and look at things
From others' points-of-view.

Bill's still got his eraser,
But he's never told his mates,
And he only rubs out pencil marks
And not the things he hates.

WELL-KNOWN SAYINGS THAT DON'T EXIST

There's smoke without a chimney.
There are balls without a game.
There are feet that have nowhere to go.
There are guests that never came.
There is traffic on a Sunday,
And you can't have Nothing Pie,
There's a C in every ocean,
And a KY in the sky.

HORACE

Much to his Mum and Dad's dismay
Horace ate himself one day.
He didn't stop to say his grace,
He just sat down and ate his face.
'We can't have this!' his Dad declared,
'If that lad's ate, he should be shared.'
But even as he spoke they saw
Horace eating more and more:
First his legs, and then his thighs,
His arms, his nose, his hair, his eyes . . .
'Stop him, someone!' Mother cried,
'Those eyeballs would be better fried!'
But all too late! And now the silly
Had even started on his willy!
'Oh Foolish child!' the father mourns,
'You could have deep-fried that with prawns,

'Some parsley and some tartare sauce . . .'
But H. was on his second course:
His liver and his lights and lung,
His ears, his neck, his chin, his tongue . . .
'To think I raised him from the cot,
And now he's going to scoff the lot!'
His Mother cried, 'What shall we do?
What's left won't even make a stew!'
And as she wept, her son was seen
To eat his head, his heart, his spleen.
And there he lay – a boy no more –
Just a stomach on the floor . . .
But none the less, since it *was* his,
They ate it – that's what haggis is. *

* *No it isn't. Haggis is a kind of stuffed pudding eaten by the Scots. The minced heart, liver, lungs of a sheep, calf or other animal's inner organs are mixed with oatmeal, sealed and boiled in the maw (intestinal stomach-bag) of a sheep and . . . excuse me a minute. Ed.*

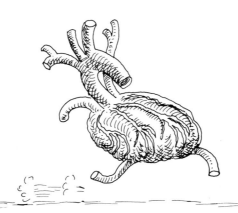

DOROTHY JANE

Dorothy Jane
Fell out of a plane
Though the reasons are still far from clear.
She was heard to complain
And complain and complain,
Though of what I have just no idea.

Dorothy Jane
Would complain and complain
About everything under the sun.
She'd complain and complain
And complain and complain –
She thought that complaining was fun.

'My seat belt's too tight!
I don't want my light!
I hate mayonnaise on my eggs!
I don't like this flight!
The sun is too bright!
And why have I only *two* legs?'

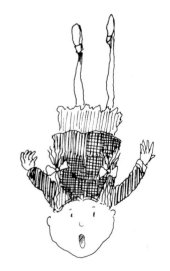

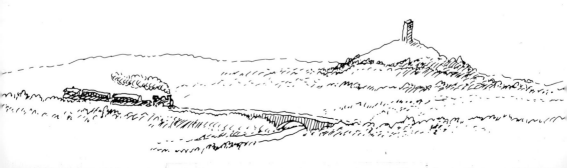

Dorothy Jane,
I'm afraid, was a pain
In the neck, in the side, in the head.
She'd complain and complain
And complain and complain
Until most people wished she were dead.

'I'm not feeling well!
What is that smell?
Why are we flying so low?
Why've you opened the door?
What's this hole in the floor?
The emergency exit? Uh-oh!'

Dorothy Jane
Fell out of a plane,
Though the reasons are still far from clear.
She was wont to complain
And complain and complain
Though she recently hasn't, I hear.

MOULDY LAND

In Mouldy Land
In Mouldy Land
They buy their mice in tins.
They race elastic bandages,
And shoot whoever wins.

The shops are full of cobweb pies.
The buses have bad feet.
They've Homes For Eaten Sandwiches,
Dead-ends to every street.

And yet the people there live well
– As far as they can see –
As long as they've got treacle farts
And buttered bums for tea.

SOLDIERS

If you're feeling jaded,
Or if you're feeling blue,
Have a little battle . . .
That's what the soldiers do.

When Genghis Khan was feeling bored
He'd gather up his Golden Horde
And say: 'Today we'll devastate
As far as Kiev.' And they'd say: 'Great!'

A Khan who wants to bring some charm
Into his life will spread some harm.
A little killing, here and there,
Gives life to armies everywhere.

It's very hard, you see, to train
For years in ways of causing pain
Without occasionally trying
Out the latest ways of dying.

The Goths, when life began to pall,
Would simply go and ravage Gaul.
And every Vandal, every Hun,
Agreed on 'How To Have Some Fun'.

Caesar and Napoleon too
Would all do what good soldiers do,
And – who knows? – get a little thrill
From giving chaps the chance to kill.

So if you're feeling jaded,
Or if you're feeling blue,
Have a little battle . . .
That's what the soldiers do.

A SCOTTISH MYSTERY

'Twas on a dirk an' stormy nicht,
The Widow an' her otter
Were seated roun' the fire sae bricht,
When someone came an' gotter!

They wondred *why*? They wondred *who*?
They wondred *how* he'd hit her,
But as they wondred what to *do* . . .
They heard the otter *titter*!

It tittered once, it tittered thrice.
It rolled aroun' the floor.
It started laughing out aloud . . .
An' then it laughed some more!

It clutched its sides an' howled wi' glee!
An' the Widow? – och! They forgot her . . .
They stood in awe – struck dumb to see
That helpless, laughing otter.

It shrieked wi' mirth. It split its sides . . .
The tears ran to its eyes.
An' then it stopt, an' walked awa'
Much to their surprise.

An' to this dee, the folks on Skye
Say they dinna ken the half . . .
Wha' made ol' Widow Braidie die!
Wha' made the otter *laugh*!

THE DAY THE ANIMALS TALKED

I woke up one morning
When the sun was high,
And I thought: 'Something's up!'
Though I didn't know why.

I got out of bed,
Then I went white as chalk,
For I suddenly heard
My goldfish talk.

'Ah! You've got up at last!
And about time!' it said.
I've been swimming all night,
While you've been in bed!'

Well! You can imagine
My utter surprise;
I didn't believe
My ears or my eyes.

I was going to exclaim:
'Did *I* hear *you* talk?'
But just then the dog said:
'I need a walk!'

I turned and saw Rover
(Imagine the shock)
As he said: 'A good long one –
Not once round the block!'

I thought: 'This is crazy!'
But more was to come . . .
When I started to answer,
I found I was dumb!

I spluttered and pointed
And tried to say: 'Wait!'
But nothing came out,
And the cat muttered: 'Great!

'The Boss has gone mute on us!
Just what we need!
How's he going to buy catfood?'
'And what about seed?'

This was the budgie,
Pacing its cage,
And who all of a sudden
Flew into a rage:

'Lemme out! You sadist!'
It pecked at its bell.
'I can't bear this prison!
My life here is hell!'

I tried to say 'Sorry!'
But nothing came out,
Then it was the goldfish
Who'd started to shout:

'What about me?
I'm stuck in this bowl
With nowhere to hide
Not so much as a hole!

'Don't you think *I* go crazy?
I'm stared at all day
By that monster!' But Ginger
The cat looked away.

And I tried to say: 'Pets!
Please listen to me!'
But I was as dumb
As *they'd* been previously.

'You listen to us,
For a change!' said a mouse
Who appeared on a cupboard
'We live in this house,

'Yet you fill it with traps,
And you poison my young!'
And the others all murmured:
'He ought to be hung!'

But Rover stood by me,
And said: 'Listen here!
It may be the Master
Has just no idea

'Of half of the things
That go on in his name . . .'
The cat said: 'Let's show him!'
The rest said: 'We're game!'

So the animals dragged me
By beak and by paw
To the zoo, and I couldn't
Believe what I saw:

All the cages were open
The creatures roamed free,
And walked on their hind legs
Like you and like me.

When they saw me, they started
To scream: 'One's got loose!'
That's a dangerous animal!'
Clamoured a goose.

'They've cooked all my ancestors,
Thousands a year!'
'And mine!' cried a bison.
'And mine!' sighed a deer.

And the animals started
To bellow and roar,
Till the lion held up
An immaculate paw:

'Now listen! A lot of us
Hunt for our meat.
This creature's no different.
His kind have to eat.'

'But they torture us, Lion!'
The goose again crowed.
'They force us to feed
Till our livers explode!'

'Is this *possible*, Man?'
The lion turned to me,
And I couldn't deny it
(Nor could I agree).

And the murmur of horror
Turned into a roar,
As the leopard sprang up
And growled: 'I hate him more!

'At least the Man eats
The geese that he kills –
My kind he pursues
For his fashions and frills!'

'That's right!' cried the mink
And the seals and the bears.
'Who wants to be murdered
For something *he* wears?'

'And us, dears!' the musk deer
Were whispering as well.
'We're slaughtered merely
Cause men like our smell!'

'Ah! My friends! This is nothing!'
The fox had begun,
'Men hunt us poor foxes
Simply for *fun*!'

The babble of voices
Arose to the skies,
And the Lion turned to me
With tears in his eyes.

'Oh, Man!' he said sadly,
'What have you to say?'
And I stood there as dumb
As a bottle of hay.

'Make him into a hand-bag!'
The crocodiles croaked.
'Turn him into a hat-stand,'
The elephants joked.

And the lion said: 'Oh, Man!
How *could* you have done
All these terrible things
By the light of the sun?

'You're found to be guilty!
You have no excuse,
And your punishment shall
Be pronounced by the goose!'

Then the animals bickered
And cried: 'No! Let me!'
But the Goose cackled: 'Listen!
Here's what it shall be!

'Let's leave him to stew
On his own for a bit,
Then we'll pluck him and gut him
To roast on the spit!'

But the rest started screeching
With different ideas,
And I dropped to my knees,
With my hands on my ears.

Then I felt myself lifted
And thrown in a cage,
And I lay there in terror
For what seemed an age . . .

I awoke all alone.
Above me – the stars –
When I suddenly heard
A quiet tap on the bars,

And there was old Rover
At my cage's doors,
Concern in his eyes
And a key in his jaws.

'Come on, Master,' he grumbled,
While everyone sleeps,
'Let's get out of here
– this place gives me the creeps!'

He opened the cage
And I licked his dear face,
And I kept close to heel,
For I felt in disgrace.

And when we got home,
He put me to bed
Under the table,
And gently he said:

'Goodnight, old fellow.'
In his kindly tone,
And he patted my head,
And he gave me a bone.

And I settled right down,
And I slept like a log,
Thinking: 'Golly! I'm happy
I'm only a dog!'

EXTINCTION DAY

The Dodo and the Barbary Lion,
The Cuban Yellow Bat,
The Atlas Bear, the Quagga and
The Christmas Island Rat,
The Thylacine, the Blue Buck
And the Hau Kuahiwi plant
Have all one thing in common now,
And that is that they aren't.

Give me one good reason why,
I wonder if you can?
The answer's in a single word –
The word is simply: Man.

Extinction Day, Extinction Day,
It isn't all that far away
For many animals and birds.
So let us decimate the herds,
Let's hunt their eggs and spoil their land,
Let's give Extinction a Big Hand,
For when it comes, it's here to stay . . .
Extinction Day! Extinction Day!

CUBAN
YELLOW
BAT

HAU KUAHIWI

ATLAS BEAR.

BLUE BUCK

THYLACINE

DODO   (Mauritius). Exterminated by Dutch colonists c. 1680.

BARBARY LION   (North Africa). The deforestation of North Africa, begun by the Romans to feed their Empire, reduced much of the area to desert. The destruction of its habitat combined with hunting wiped out the lion by around 1922.

CUBAN YELLOW BAT   (Cuba). Became extinct c. 1850.

ATLAS BEAR   (North Africa). Suffered like the Barbary Lion from the destruction of its habitat by man. The last Atlas Bear was hunted down c. 1870.

QUAGGA   (South Africa). It was hunted to extinction for its skins. The last one died in the Amsterdam Zoo in 1883.

THE CHRISTMAS ISLAND RAT   (Christmas Island, Indian Ocean). Two rats unique to this island, Captain Maclear's Rat and the Bulldog Rat, were wiped out by disease in about nine years, after a mining settlement was established c. 1900.

THYLACINE   (Tasmania). Otherwise known as the Tasmanian Wolf, it was deliberately hunted down by the Government in the nineteenth century. The last one died in Hobart Zoo in 1933.

BLUE BUCK   (Cape Colony, S. Africa). Hunted to extinction by settlers. The last one was shot c. 1799.

HAU KUAHIWI   (Hawaii). The coming of the Europeans began the extinction of birds called Honeycreepers, on which the Hau Kuahiwi depended for pollination. As the birds died out so too did the Hau Kuahiwi c. 1912.

For more on this subject see David Day's fascinating book: The Doomsday Book of Animals, *1981 (Ebury Press, London).*

BARBARY LION   QUAGGA   CHRISTMAS ISLAND RAT   DODO

THE GRUMBLE-WHEEZER TREE

Did you ever see
A Grumble-Wheezer tree?
It's a really most extraordinary sight.
All its leaves are shaped like hats
And its trunk is full of rats,
And it wanders round the town at dead of night.

It lurks in alleyways
Throwing cans at passing strays,
And frightening lonely policemen on the beat.
And it sometimes sits for hours
Playing cards with wilting flowers
(Though the Grumble-Wheezer always seems to cheat).

It'll sometimes settle down
On the wrong side of the town,
With a can of beer to watch an old TV.
And it doesn't really care,
If the cats come round to stare,
Or even if a dog comes for a pee.

But the thing it cannot stand
Is a military band
Playing marches in that hearty sort of way.
If it hears a single note
It'll go straight for their throat
Or else chase them till they promise not to play.

So if you are about
When the Grumble-Wheezer's out
Just be careful where you wander in the dark.
It'll grab you by the hair
And tear off your underwear
And then arrange it (rather rudely) round the Park.

ALGERNON THE VIKING

Algernon the Viking
Had a funny sort of nose,
The sort that grows and grows
And grows and grows and grows.

When he was just a youngster,
Learning crime and doing wrong,
His olfactory organ
Was already two feet long.

His Mother said: 'It's lovely!'
But his Dad said: 'He's a freak.
I'll go and steal another
Child with a more standard beak.'

But his Mother wouldn't lose him,
And she gave him lots to eat,
So that by the time he'd reached
Six foot – his nose had reached his feet!

The girls all sniggered at him,
Called him 'Nosey Algernon',
And all he could reply was:
'Pnease! Nind what nyou're stnanding on!'

Then his Father built a warship
Saying: 'Let's go raiding, Chums!
Although guess who isn't in
The crew – no matter who else comes?'

Algy pleaded with his
Dad, but the reply was: 'No!
A conk like that is just
A drag – especially when we row.'

'No, it's lovely!' said his Mum,
'And if he lies flat on his back,
You can use his snozzle as
The mast – now go and help him pack.'

So the ship set off plus Algy
With the sail fixed to his nose
– A-turning and a-twisting
Catching every wind that blows.

And they'd never sailed so surely,
And they'd never sailed so fast,
As when Algernon the Viking's nose
Was turned into the mast.

Then they landed somewhere foreign,
Algy's Dad said: 'You stay here.
I'll not have our victims laugh
At us – they're meant to scream with fear.'

'Nonsense!' said his Mother
(Who enjoyed a trip at sea)
'You let him go and fight
With you, while I prepare the tea.'

So the Vikings leapt out screaming,
Curdling blood and frightening foes,
And Algy boldly followed with
His extraordinary nose.

And though he was behind
The rest, his nose stuck out ahead,
Complete with hairs and pimples
Yellow, pink and puce and red.

And Algy fought behind it
(Though he'd got a nasty cough)
And he chose to fight the fiercest
Foes – so they could cut it off.

But the enemy was stricken
When they saw that mighty trunk,
And they cried: 'St. Patrick save us!'
And did History's quickest bunk.

But just as one was running,
He returned with cut and thrust,
And he sliced right through young Algy's
Nose, and it fell down in the dust.

Algy toppled backwards,
For his balance was put out,
And he fell into a swoon
Now disencumbered of his snout.

Well the Vikings were victorious,
And they held a Victory Tea,
But Algy's Mum was shattered
When she saw her son nose-free.

'Oh, Algy! It were lovely!
Your proboscis was my joy,
And now,' she cried, '*look* at you!
You're just like *any other boy*!'

And his Dad was really livid.
He began to rant and rail.
'You stupid little blighter!
Now we haven't got a sail!'

And so they had to row
Back home, leaving Algy there,
Feeling glad he'd lost his hooter,
But that Life was not quite fair.

THE BOLDIMUN & THE IG

'What's the best method of keeping an Ig?'
The Boldimun asked a passing pig.
The Pig looked up and he sniffed the air,
And he said: 'Igs like to be scratched just *there*.
Give it lots of slops and some bits of rind,
And your Ig'll be happy, I think you'll find.'

So the Boldimun turned to his Ig and he said:
'Then that's what I'll do!' BUT THE IG SHOOK ITS HEAD.

'I've an Ig,' said the Boldimun
To a dog that was lying there out in the sun.
'How should I keep it? Tell me please?'
The Dog looked up and it scratched its fleas
And said 'Give it a bone and a daily run
And your Ig'll think that its life is fun.'

So the Boldimun turned to the Ig and he said:
'Then *that's* what I'll do!' BUT THE IG SHOOK ITS HEAD.

'Oh what shall I do?' the Boldimun cried
To a crocodile down by the waterside.
'I've an Ig I must keep, but I don't know how!'
And the Crocodile grinned and he said: 'Right now,
Your Ig would like you to climb on my back.'
So the Boldimun did, and the Croc went 'Snack!'

And he swallowed the Boldimun whole and said:
'How's that?' AND THE IG NODDED ITS HEAD.

IF ALL THE STARS IN HEAVEN

If all the stars in heaven
Were made of Katto-meat,
I bet our cat would still make-out
He'd not enough to eat!

If I were filled with rubbish,
And all I spoke was birds,
I'd never eat my heart out
– Though I might eat my words.

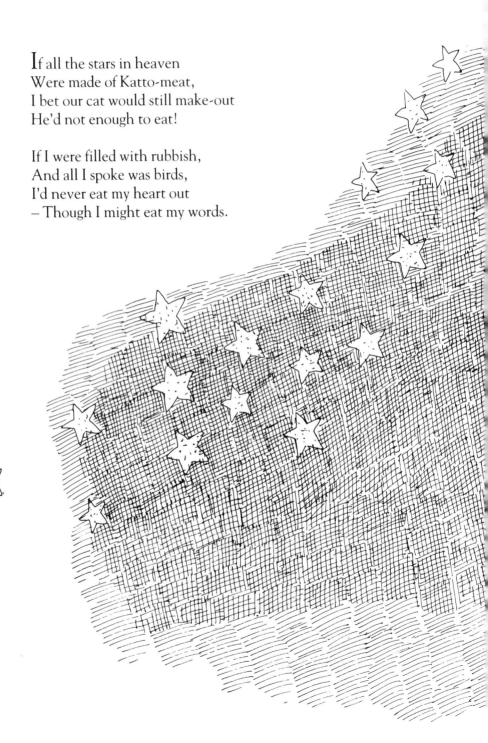

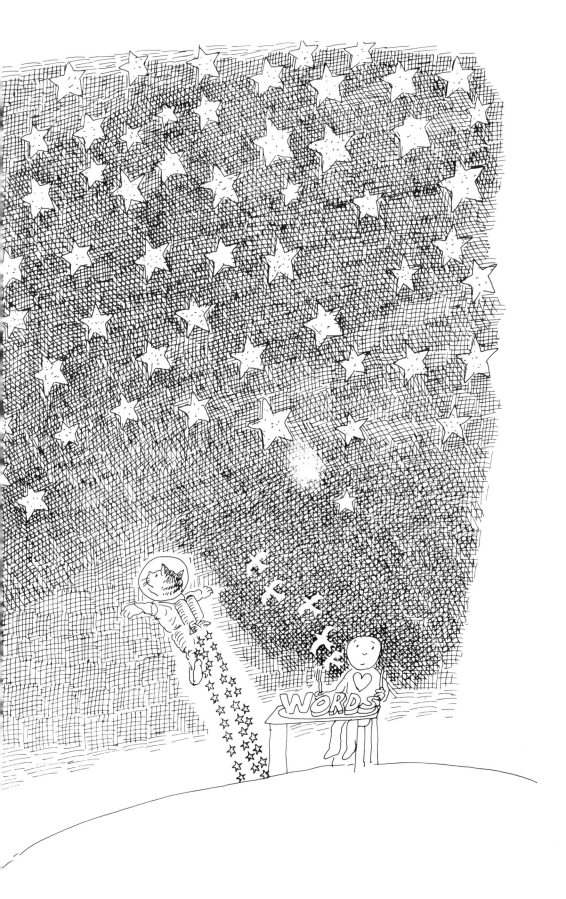

THE EXPERTS

Give three cheers for experts,
They know a thing or two,
And if we didn't have 'em
Whatever would we do?

They built a ship that couldn't sink;
It sailed across the sea.
It's name was *The Titanic* –
It's gone down in history.

For years and years the experts knew
The Sun went round the Earth,
And when Copernicus said: 'Wrong!'
They couldn't hide their mirth.

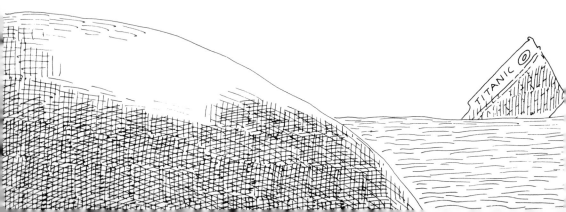

They told Columbus not to sail
Because he might fall off.
They had King Louis bled to death,
Because he'd got a cough.

Lord Kelvin was a scientist –
A *really* clever guy,
Who proved by mathematics
That man would *never* fly.

And now we've all got nuclear power
So give three mighty cheers –
The experts say it can't go wrong
Once in ten thousand years!

THE EMPEROR'S SECRET

The Secret of the Emperor Dan
Was known to EVERY LIVING MAN,
For anyone who came to tea
Could see it – plain as it could be –
In the middle of the room,
Illuminated in the gloom.
There it drew astonished eyes
With labels of enormous size
Which gave instructions for its use,
And 'What to do' if it got loose.
There was a brush and pots of glue
To stick on what fell off, and you
Could see the dirt behind its ears
Must have been there for years and years,
And now was neatly planted out
With rows of beans. And, if in doubt,
The curious visitor would find
The Emperor creep up from behind
And grab his arm, and say: 'I see
You know my Secret now!' And he
Would start to cry and say: 'I know
It's not too good – as secrets go –

'Since everybody on this Planet
Seems to know about it – damn it!
But I don't care! I really don't!
You think I'll swap it? No I won't!
For that's *my* Secret – like it, like it not –
And *it's the only one I've got!*
Oh! How I envy those who keep
A thousand secrets – just like sheep.
Or kings and queens and lords and such
Who keep *their* secrets in a hutch.
But I cannot! For – you can tell –
I like to keep my Secret well!
Some folks keep secrets in the dark,
Well I say: Stuff that for a lark!
I like to see my Secret out,
Gadding around and free from doubt!
I like to see it large as life,
Admired alike by man and wife.
I like to see it living free,
Untrammelled by the likes of me,
For I – a puny mortal am
And that's *my* Secret . . . it's called Sam.'

INVALUABLE ADVICE

Never shower in treacle
That would be my advice;
It probably won't harm you,
But it isn't very nice.

And never wear a chicken –
Not even round your chin!
It's not they're just not fashionable,
But they make *such* a din!

Don't be hard on broccoli
No matter what they've done,
And never leave your insides out
To fester in the sun.

Never niggle ocelots
Nor bare your soul to hake,
And sticking Catholic priests to geese
With glue *is* a mistake.

Don't invent the motor car,
And don't buy shares in Mice,
And *never* lick a rhino's ear . . .
It's all Invaluable Advice!

MY BEST ICE-CREAM

The best ice-cream
I think I've ever tasted
Was the one I fell in
When I was only ten.
It was huge, I tell you –
The size of a small mountain,
And there is no telling
When we'll see its likes again.

The best stick of rock
I think I've ever eaten
Was the one I climbed up
When I was only four.
It took six days,
Then I started eating downwards
And when midnight chimed
I had gnawed it to the floor!

The best fizzy drink
I think I've ever swallowed
Was the one I sailed across
When I was only eight.
It was wide across
As the great Pacific Ocean,
And I drank it with an albatross
Whose name was Kate.

BLACK JACK ATKINS

Pirates come and pirates go,
But Black Jack Atkins doesn't – no!
He wanders still the Spanish Main
– Without a leg – without a brain
– Without a chest – without a head
In fact – officially – he's dead,
So what I said before was wrong,
Poor Black Jack Atkins is long gone –
I wonder why I took the time
To write quite *such* a pointless rhyme?

PET FOOD

What do you get, Jude,
When you eat Pet Food?

Hamsterburgers,
Poodle Pies,
Goldfish Fingers,
Canary Fries.

Budgie Bangers,
Dachshunds and Mash,
Pickled Parrots,
Corned Cat Hash.

Gerbils on Toast,
Tortoise Teas,
Horse-in-a-basket,
Mice and Peas.

That's what you get, Jude,
When you eat Pet Food!

A NEW ATTEMPT ON THE
WORLD RHYMING CHAMPIONSHIP RECORD!

A panto-writer, Harry Hyam,
Who was extremely fond of rhyme,
One day said to his comrades: 'I'm
Just sick of writing pantomime
For which I get paid half a dime,
I'm going to write a poem sublime,
By which you'll see my fame will climb
Above all others, for this time
I'm only going to use ONE rhyme!'
His friends said he was past his prime
And even working overtime,
They said, he'd never keep ONE rhyme
Right through a poem. But Harry Hyam
Had started off, and by noontime
He'd written fifteen lines of rhyme
Each one the same, and by teatime

He'd written more and more, betime.
But listen! Isn't it a crime?
It happened that a small enzyme*
That looked like just a speck of lime
Had landed on his hand some time,
And as he heard the midnight chime
This enzyme started making slime
That smelt of matters maritime,
And oozed out through his fingers' grime
And landed on his paper. I'm
Quite sure I do not need to mime
What happened next, but, by bedtime,
This slime and grime had caused a zyme**
Which wholly covered Harry Hyam,
And, as he lived in Hildesheim
Which has a hot and sultry clime

(Especially in the summertime),
This zyme converted into chyme***
And soon digested Harry Hyam
From slimy feet to slimy cyme,****
His hands, his hair, his pen, his rhyme.
And all it left was half a dime
They'd paid him for the pantomime
They put on once in Burgwindheim.
His friends came round at breakfast time,
And sighed to find this paradigm
For poets gone. The half a dime
They took and tied it up in sime*****
And buried it in Gudelsheim.
And on the grave they planted thyme
– For that's all there was left to rhyme.

*Enzyme: *Any of a class of complex organic substances that cause chemical transformations of material in plants and animal; formerly called 'ferment'.*

**Zyme: *The substance causing a zymotic disease. (Zymotic: A general epithet for infectious diseases, originally because they were regarded as being caused by a process analogous to fermentation.)*

***Chyme: *The semi-fluid pulpy acid matter into which food is converted in the stomach by the action of the gastric secretion.*

*****Cyme: *A head (from the French cyme or cime, meaning 'top', 'summit').*

******Sime: *A rope or chord. (A northern dialect word last recorded in 1899 and which is now to be found only in rhyming dictionaries.)*

IF DEAD LEAVES WERE MONEY

If dead leaves were money,
I'd never be broke.
If troubles were funny,
We'd all share a joke.

THE CURSE OF THE VAMPIRE'S SOCKS

The vampire lay dead,
Transfixed in his box.
The townsfolk stood round him,
Transfixed by his socks,
For though the old count
Lay there dead as a bun,
His socks had both started
To shine like the sun.
And a voice from the grave
Cried: 'Fools! Now you can see
That you can't kill my socks,
Though you may have killed me!'

The townsfolk in terror
All ran from that sight,
But the socks rose above them
And lit up the night.
And the people all shuddered,
And doubled their locks,
Wondering *what* was the curse
Of the old vampire's socks?
But all the night long
Those socks hung in the sky,
Lighting the world,
And the world wondered: 'Why?'

'It isn't *so* bad,'
Said the Mayor of the Town.
'It means we can close
All the street-lighting down.'
Then the nightwatchman said:
'Well they're good news for *me*,
For while I'm on duty
They mean I can see!'
And kids and insomniacs
Quickly agreed
By the light of those socks
They could sit out and read!

But the next day the matter
Took a turn for the worse,
And they started to fathom
The old Vampire's Curse,
For as the sun shone
And rose high in the sky,
The old Vampire's socks
Both started to fry.
And as it got hotter
Folk knew what was wrong,
For the old Vampire's socks
Had started to pong!

The day was a scorcher.
The temperature rose,
And so did the stench
From those heels and those toes.
The townspeople tried
To keep shut up indoors,
But the smell from those socks
Came up through the floors,
And it squeezed in the cracks
Of the shutters and still
It got stronger and stronger
Till they all felt quite ill.

The Mayor screamed: 'They're lethal!
We must get them down!'
And then he threw-up
On his mayorial gown.
'Who's got a ladder?'
'Who's got a lasso?'
They cried out, but no one
Could think what to do.
And those socks simply hung there
And smelt worse and worse,
And the townspeople rued
The old Vampire's Curse.

The townsfolk grew iller.
They all took to bed,
And they didn't go shopping;
They didn't bake bread.
The dustbins weren't emptied.
The drains over-flowed,
Till the town itself stank
From each alley and road.
'I'll offer this gold,'
Said the Mayor with a sigh,
'To the man who can get
Those socks out of the sky!'

Market Day came,
And the stench was so rife
That no one was out
Except one farmer's wife.
She went to the Mayor,
And she said 'Hello, dear!
I'll get rid of those socks
For us all – never fear!'
The Mayor groaned: 'I've offered
This gold to the man
Who can do it. I very much
Doubt if *you* can!'

But the Farmer's Wife chuckled.
'Don't worry your head,
My dearie! You just stay here
Tucked up in bed.'
Then she climbed on her goose
And she told it to fly
Straight up to those socks
That still stank in the sky.
When she reached them she filled them
With garlic and chives,
And then brought them to earth
Like a cat with nine lives.

Next she filled them with milk,
And hung them to drain
Over a basin.
Then she filled them again.
The Mayor said: 'They still smell
As bad – you'll agree?'
The Farmer's Wife answered:
'Just leave it to me.'
And she worked with a will,
And she worked at her ease,
Till the Farmer's Wife made
Those socks into a cheese.

Then she cut it in slices,
And handed it out
To all of the townsfolk
Who'd gathered about.
'But it smells!' they cried,
And they waggled their ears.
She said: 'Just have a nibble –
You'll like it, my dears!'
Then the Mayor said: '*I'll* try!'
And he ate up a slice,
And he thought for a moment,
Then he said: 'Very nice!'

Then the others all tried it,
And said: 'It's a breeze!
We're really quite partial
To Vampire Sock Cheese!'
And they found once they'd eaten
The cheese, none could tell
If the old Vampire's socks
Still continued to smell.
Then the Farmer's Wife said
To the Mayor: 'Now then, Dear,
How about that reward?'
But the Mayor said: 'No fear!

'You'll make a small fortune
From that cheese – if you can.
Besides, the reward
Was to go to a *man!*'
The Farmer's Wife frowned
And she said: 'Oh, my Dear,
You shouldn't go back
On a promise, I fear.'
But the Mayor wouldn't listen
And said: 'Run along!'
And he had her thrown out . . .
Now I think this was wrong.

For the Farmer's Wife took
Her cheese to the box
Where the Vampire still lay
(Although minus his socks)
And she put the cheese under
His nose for so long
That he opened his eyes
On account of the pong.
'Good Grief!' cried the Vampire,
His eyes glowing red,
'That cheese is enough
To awaken the dead!'

'Now, my Dear,' said the Farmer's Wife,
'Go to the Mayor
And tell that young fellow
He's got to play fair!'
But the Vampire leapt out
With a terrible cry,
And said: 'Those who have eaten
My socks have to die!'
'Don't be so silly!'
She said. 'You be good,
And perhaps I might help you
To reach Hollywood!'

So the Vampire rushed off
And he haunted the Mayor
Till he gave that good woman
The whole of her share.
Then she took out the stake
From the old Vampire's chest,
And she bought two plane tickets,
And they headed out West.
There they both live,
With a socking great car,
And the Vampire's become
A big movie star.

He's cured, I am told,
Of his blood-sucking fits,
But he still frightens folk
Almost out of their wits –
But it's only in films
And it's only to tease.
As for the townsfolk –
They went on making cheese,
And so, I believe,
It is made to this day,
From those very same socks
In the very same way.

THE WHALER

A whaler was a-whaling
In the deep North Sea,
Wiping out endangered species
As busy as could be.

They didn't give a tootle
What sort of whales they shot:
Bowheads, Humpbacks, Sperm and Blue Whales –
They simply bagged the lot!

Mother whales and babies
– They'd no time for regrets –
They slaughtered whole herds at a time
To sell as food for pets.

When suddenly they saw a whale
Bigger than the rest,
And the Captain yelled: 'Let's get her, boys!
She's got to be the best!'

So they started chasing after
That extraordinary whale,
And they didn't stop their engines
Till they'd caught up with its tail,

Then they fired off their harpoon,
With its explosive head,
And the thing exploded in the beast
And should have killed it dead.

But the creature thrashed and turned on them,
And gave a sort of 'cluck!',
And the Captain screamed: 'That's not a whale!
My boys! It's Moby Duck!'

But Moby Duck closed in on them
– Rage written on his face –
His huge beak snapping at their stern,
As they began to race.

He chased them through the North Sea,
There was nothing they could do,
For he caught them and in moments
He had pecked their boat in two.

They scrambled for the lifeboats,
And they lived to tell the tale,
But those whalers never ever
Tried to kill another whale.

And what of Moby Duck, my friends?
Ah! but who can say?
He swam into the sunset
To quack another day.

THE NEW MIND

The wind blew through my head
And blew my mind away,
And as I watched my mind fly off
I thought I heard it say:

'I've got to cross mountains!
I've got to cross the sea!
I can't stand bodies any more!
I'm going to be free!'

And it was gone! Like . . . that !
And I was left behind.
I couldn't even wonder what
I'd do without a mind.

I just stood there – a body.
I couldn't see or talk.
I had no thoughts. I had no hopes.
I couldn't sit or walk.

Other winds blew through me,
And I did not resist.
Looking back, I wonder, did I
Actually exist?

But something happened next
That was extraordinary:
Another mind blew in my head
So I could think and see.

But as I looked around me,
Though everything looked fine,
I knew the mind the wind had brought me
Wasn't really mine.

It took me up a hillside,
And then it took me down,
And when I saw the Sun shine bright
It simply made me frown.

'What's the trouble, Darling?'
The Sun inquired of me,
And – to my own amazement – I said:
'Everything is *free*!'

'No one's making money
Out of all these precious things!
There's no charge for the air we breathe
Or for what the skylark sings!

'The grass is green for nothing.
You always shine as bright
On everybody – rich or poor –
Now, surely, that's not right?

'It *can't* be right for everyone
Regardless of their wealth
To see the world so beautiful
And to enjoy good health!

'The sky is blue for all!
And there's no charge for the sea!
Well! What's the point of being rich
If things like *that* are free?'

The Sun looked rather niggled
(Though he still tried to be kind)
He shook his head and sadly said:
'You must have lost your mind!'

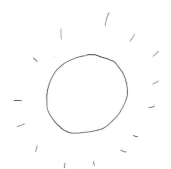

And I *had*! But I ignored him,
For I was laying down
Concrete for a car park and
Foundations for a town.

At length I heard the Sun shout:
'Hey! Sweetheart! I mean *you*!
To make a town you must have people!'
I replied: 'That's true.'

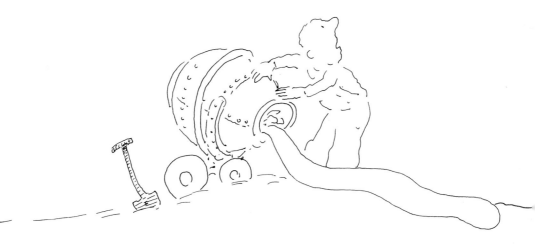

My new mind then amazed me
For it made me fix a sign
Reading: 'POTS OF GOLD ARE BURIED HERE!
APPLICANTS STAND IN LINE!'

And sure enough in no time
There were queues of young and old
Prepared to live in concrete
To gain a pot of gold.

And some of them made money
From all the others there,
But most lived in damp basements
Far away from light and air.

And the Sun said: 'Are they happy?'
My mind replied: 'Search me . . .
But watch how wealthy I can get
Out of their poverty!

'Now I can charge for sunshine!
For if they want a room
That sees you, Sun, they must pay more
Or else stay in the gloom!

'And if they want a garden
While trying to amass
Their fortunes, they must pay for one . . .
I'll charge them for the grass!'

The Sun just winked and said:
'Ah, Petkins! Now I see
How simple making money is!
How happy you must be!'

'*Happy?*' said my new mind,
'That isn't what it's for!
The only point to all of this
Is making even *more*!'

And so I started building
Before the Sun could blink
Furnaces and factories
That made the breezes stink.

The air was black with smoke
That spread beyond my town
And poisoned rivers round about
And brought the forests down.

The Sun said: 'I say, Sweetie!
What's going on down there?
Your lovely spot now looks more like
Gorilla's underwear!'

My new mind said: 'Don't worry!
Everything's O.K.!
It's all so foul that now, you'll see,
They'll pay to get away!'

And so they did! By plane-fulls!
They paid to spend a week
Where it was safe to play on beaches
And the rivers didn't reek.

The Sun looked rather doubtful,
But I said: 'It's fine by me!
I've got them paying for the air
And paying for the sea.'

And that was when it happened!
Don't ask me how or why –
The Sun just got extremely hot
Till my mind began to fry.

It frizzled till it melted,
And then, when I lay down,
My new mind poured out of my ears
And turned my pillow brown.

And there I lay a life-time
With space inside my head,
Deprived of feelings, thoughts and hopes –
I was as good as dead.

But then, one misty morning,
There was a clicker-clack;
The window softly opened,
And my right mind tip-toed back.

'I've been across the mountains,'
It said, 'and seen the sea,
But even as I flew they changed
From what they ought to be:

'Green and grassy hill-sides,
Where trees and flowers grew,
Turned black and died, and there was not
A thing that I could do.'

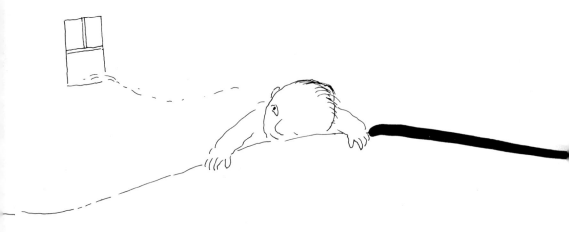

I said, when it had finished:
'Please *don't* think I'm unkind,
But you see *you* need a body, just
As *I* must have a mind.

'There's not much point in thinking
The kind of things you do,
If you haven't got a pair of hands
To help those thoughts come true.'

My mind went sort of silent,
And then it said: 'O.K.
If you won't be a drag on me,
I won't run away.'

So now we work together,
While things go from bad to worse:
I pushed this pen across this page –
My mind made up this verse.

DANCING IN THE DUST

Croesus was as rich as sin.
Cyrus and his son
Darius ruled all Persia.
Yet *now* where are they? . . . Gone.

Gone where old Pythagorus gives
The square dance symmetry,
Where Sappho springs on heels of love
Beside a tideless sea.

Where Pharaohs do the sand-dance,
And Caesar reels through Gaul,
Salome dances on ahead,
While Hadrian foots his wall.

Where Chaucer treads his country dance
With Breugel at his heel,
Sir Walter Raleigh leads Queen Bess
In a Virginia Reel.

Nelson hops his hornpipe there,
Abel jigs with Seth.
Darwin does the fox-trot,
And Poe – his Dance of Death.

While Mozart plucks from paradise
Notes so sweet and just
That all our forebears dance . . . and we
Come dancing in their dust.